Contents

Blippi™
The Great Sneaker Hunt!

Written by Meredith Rusu
Illustrated by Maurizio Campidelli

What a great party at the play center this has been! "Thanks for inviting me— Happy birthday!"

HAP

The cubby where I left my sneakers is empty!

"Uh-oh," says the attendant. "What color are they?"
"They're blue and orange," I tell her, "my favorite colors."

7

"We have a lot of blue-and-orange sneakers today," she says. "I bet someone took them by mistake."

She looks around the play center.
"Could that be them by the tumbling mats?"

Those could be my sneakers, but it's hard to tell from here. The great sneaker hunt is on!

It looks like the quickest way to the tumbling mats is across the trampolines. So it's time to do some cartwheels. One, two, three!

Gee, these aren't my sneakers!

Maybe I can spot my missing sneakers if
I bounce high enough.
Bounce, bounce, bounce!

Are those my sneakers on top of the foam pit?
If so, that's a silly place for them to be!

Hey, where'd those sneaky sneakers go?
They were on top of the foam pit just a minute ago.

Ha ha! I know what must have happened.
I bet my sneakers fell down into the pile when
the blocks moved.

You know what I have to do, right?
I have to dive in and look for my sneakers.
Here I go!

"Have you seen a pair of orange-and blue-sneakers by any chance?" I ask.

"I think we saw a pair like that over by the slide a little while ago," they say.

What better way to zoom over to the slide than by scooter?

Whee!

I don't see my sneakers anywhere!
I'm going to climb the stairs and take a really good look around.

There's nothing out there that looks like my sneakers.
You know what the fastest way down is, right?
Woah—this is fun!

24

"Hi again!" I say to the attendant.

"Look what I've got!" she says.

"My sneakers!" I shout.

"Yes! Someone did take your sneakers by mistake, and they just returned them," she says, smiling.

Hooray! I've finally got my sneakers where they belong—on my feet. Now they can walk home with me!

Blippi™

A Pet for Blippi!

Written by Marilyn Easton
Illustrated by Adam Devaney

I'm volunteering at an animal shelter today! An animal shelter is a place where pets that need homes live.

The people who work here make sure the pets are healthy and happy while they wait for their forever homes.

I can't wait to help someone find just the right pet for them!

This shelter has so many different animals that need homes. There are a lot of dogs. Some of them are big, and some of them are small. I love all dogs! Do you like dogs?

This shelter also has a lot of cats.
Check out all the cute kittens and cats.
I love cats too! Do you?

Wow! Look at all the colorful birds. Lots of bunnies live here too. Guess what? I love birds and bunnies!

There are even some turtles waiting to be adopted.
Woah, one just poked its head out of its shell!
Oh, I just love turtles!

These people want to adopt a cat. I help them find the right one for their family.

How do I do that? I introduce them to the cats and tell them a bit about each one. Then they talk to the cats and pet them and play with them.

Hooray! They find the right cat for them!

I am so happy! The cat has a new home and a new family.

What a great feeling it is to help match the right pet to the right people.

Check it out! More people are here. They want to adopt a dog. I will try to help make another good match!

Look at this dog by himself. He looks like he might want to take a walk. Okay, let's go, pup!

Wait a minute! This dog has an orange bowtie. I show him *my* orange bowtie. He looks like he is laughing. Ha, ha! Now I am laughing too. We are having a very happy walk together.

This dog also has a nametag. It says his name is Lyno.

I show Lyno *my* nametag. "My name is Blippi!" I say.

Lyno wags his tail.

Lyno and I play fetch. This is so much fun!
It feels like we are becoming friends.

You know, I really like Lyno. I think
Lyno likes me too.

Wow, I have the best idea! I'll adopt Lyno! I'll give him a forever home and take good care of him.

That means I will feed him

and brush him

and take him on walks

and play with him.

And I'll be sure to take him for checkups so he can stay healthy.

Most of all, I will love him!

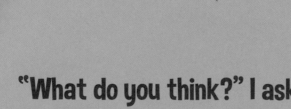

"What do you think?" I ask Lyno.
"Do you want me to adopt you?"

RUFF! Lyno says YES.

Any person who wants to adopt a pet has to talk to the people who run the shelter. There are questions to answer and forms to fill out. But then the shelter says I can adopt Lyno. Furr-tastic!

Today I came to volunteer, and now *I'm* the one leaving with a new friend.

What a great day this turned out to be— it's Lyno's Gotcha Day!

Welcome home, Lyno!

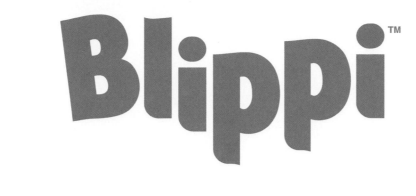

Blippi™

I Can Drive an Excavator!

Written by Marilyn Easton
Illustrated by Adam Devaney

Hey, it's me, Blippi! Look at this big digging machine! It's called an excavator.

Excavators dig into the ground at construction sites. They dig up dirt and move it away so other big machines can do their jobs.

Excavators are the best! I wish I could drive one.

Wow, my wish just came true! I am going
to drive this excavator.

An excavator works hard. All the other big machines work hard too. So will I. Watch me!

First, I need some safety equipment. I put on a hard hat and a safety vest. The hard hat will protect my head in case anything falls on or knocks into me. And do you see how brightly colored this safety vest is? That's to make sure the other construction workers can see me.

Now I am ready to sit in the excavator's cab.
It's just one step up. Make that one GIANT step!

57

Check it out! There are a lot of controls that I can use to move the excavator and its bucket.

I can't wait to get started, so I fasten my seat belt right away. *Click!*

The cab is so high up, I can see all around me. There's a lot of digging to do—here I go!

An excavator does not have wheels.
Instead, it moves on tracks. The tracks can
go over mud and rocks without getting stuck.

The ride is so nice and smooth.
Thank you, excavator tracks!

I get to the spot where I need
to dig. Then I pull the joystick to lift
the excavator's bucket up.

Now I lower the bucket, and it starts digging.
Dig, dig, dig! This part is so much fun!

When I lift the bucket, it's full of freshly dug dirt. That's so cool!

Go, excavator, go!

I drive the excavator over to a
dump truck and lower the bucket.

The dirt tumbles out and lands with a
in the bed of the dump truck.

The dump truck drives away with the dirt.
See you later, dirt!

The excavator's work is done.
Good job, excavator!

A lot of other big machines are still hard at work.

The bulldozer pushes heavy boulders out of the way.

Slosh! Slosh! The concrete mixer is mixing concrete.

The steamroller is flattening the ground,

and the crane is lifting heavy materials that need to be placed up high.

What did I help the big machines build?

A brand-new playground. It's for you!

Have fun!
I sure did.

74

Blippi™

Hello, Neighbor!

Written by Meredith Rusu
Illustrated by Maurizio Campidelli

It's a beautiful day to take a walk around my neighborhood. There are so many people to see and places to go.

"Hello, neighbors!" I call out to two people who live across the street. They wave and say hello back to me.

The people who live in your neighborhood are your neighbors. Do you know any of your neighbors?

I'm headed to one of my favorite neighborhood places. The park! Do you have a park where you live?

Look at that! These birds are each other's neighbors. They live in the same park.

I'm glad I brought birdseed. The birds are hungry today.

After I feed the birds, I head back to town. I walk past the firehouse. "Hello!" I call out to the firefighters. "Thank you for being so brave and putting out fires and saving cats stuck in trees!"

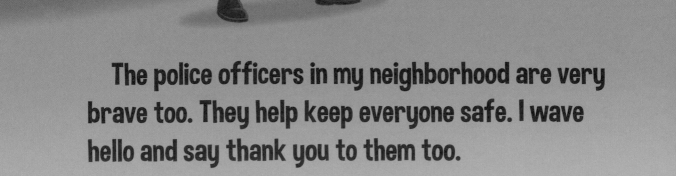

The police officers in my neighborhood are very brave too. They help keep everyone safe. I wave hello and say thank you to them too.

"Hello, Doctor!" I say at the doctor's office. "I'm here for my checkup."

Hooray! The doctor tells me I'm healthy and strong.

Next, I head over to Lyno's doctor. She's called a veterinarian, and she gives me vitamins for Lyno. They will help keep *him* healthy and strong too.

Do you know what else keeps us healthy and strong?
Good food, like lots of fruits and vegetables.

I swing by the grocery store to get some yummy things for dinner. Do you like to go to the grocery store in your neighborhood?

Wow! Check out all those amazing cakes and other sweet treats in the bakery's window. They look delicious!

There's a flower shop right next door to the bakery. Everything inside both stores smells so good.

This is the best-smelling block in the whole neighborhood!

My neighborhood has a school.

Some of the students are in the playground for recess. That means it's almost time for lunch. All of this walking has made me kind of hungry!

At the neighborhood diner, I order my favorite sandwich. "Thank you," I say to the server.

After lunch, I continue on my walk.
Jingle, jingle! Hold on! That's the sound of an ice cream truck. I really love ice cream. Do you like ice cream?

I have just a couple more places to go in my neighborhood today. First is the library. It's a very busy and very quiet place, filled with amazing books to read.

I look through the shelves and find an interesting book I want to read. I love books! Do you have a favorite book?

The last place I go in my neighborhood is the doggy day-care center. It's a very busy and very *noisy* place.

It's also where my best friend, Lyno, spent
the day today. I am so happy to see him!

Let's go home, Lyno! Our house is my favorite place in the entire neighborhood. What's yours?

Blippi™

If I Were a Dinosaur!

Written by Meredith Rusu

Illustrated by Adam Devaney

Hey, Lyno! I had so much fun today. I spent the entire day at the dinosaur museum.

There were lots of different kinds of dinosaurs
on exhibit, and I tried to see them all!

Gee, I wonder. What if *I* were a dinosaur? What kind would I be? Maybe I'd be like Allosaurus and have huge feet!

I'd get to stomp around and leave footprints wherever I went.

Stomp! Stomp! Stomp!

If I were a dinosaur, maybe I would have a long neck.
Brontosaurus had a really long neck.

Bronotsaurus had a really long tail too!
What if I had one of those?

Some dinosaurs, like Velociraptor, were super speedy.

They ran really fast, especially when they were looking for something to eat!

I love to run fast. Come on, Lyno, race you to the kitchen!

Spinosaurus and some of the other dinosaurs
I saw today had really sharp teeth.

It helps to have sharp teeth when you're hungry—and I'm hungry right now!
Lyno, it looks like you're hungry too!

Maybe I'd fly, like Pteranodon did! Pteranodon spread its giant wings and flew all around.

Let's spread our wings and fly, Lyno!

If I were a dinosaur, I wonder if I would have three horns like Triceratops. I bet those horns came in handy if Triceratops ever got into a fight! I just like them because they look so amazing!

What do you think, Lyno? Do I look like Triceratops? Do I look amazing?

Some of the biggest dinosaurs only ate plants.
If I were a dinosaur, I would be a plant-eater,
like Stegosaurus.

I love fresh veggies, especially
the ones I grow myself!

Did you know that all dinosaurs hatched from eggs? And the eggs were humongous. Some of them were the size of watermelons!

Imagine hatching from an egg.
Craaaack!
Here I am, world!

Guess what? If I were a dinosaur, I think the best part would be that I'd get to ROAR a lot, just like Tyrannosaurus rex did.

Roar with me, Lyno.

ROOOOAR!

Wow! It was great to see so many dinosaurs today and to *be* so many of them too!

What kind of dinosaur would *you* be?

Blippi™

A Good Day to Play!

Written by Marilyn Easton
Illustrated by Adam Devaney

Today is a great day to play in the park. Lyno and I love to come to the park on a nice sunny day and play ball. Go fetch, Lyno!

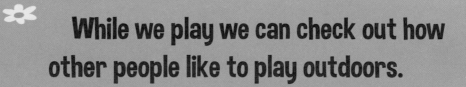

While we play we can check out how other people like to play outdoors.

The swing is so cool, especially when you get a good push!

Playing in the sandbox is a lot of fun, especially when a friend joins you. Then you get to play with their toys and share your own!

These friends are playing hide-and-seek.
Whoever stays hidden the longest is the winner!

Have you ever played hide-and-seek?
Which do you like best, hiding or seeking?

These two friends are about to race. Ready. Set. Go!

These friends are drawing with sidewalk chalk. I see
a lot of orange-and-blue drawings. Orange and blue
are my favorite colors! What's *your* favorite color?

Woah, that's one amazing slide!

These friends are having a great time climbing up the steps and then sliding down.

Oh, I just love "Simon Says!" Everyone has to listen to the leader really carefully and do what they say.

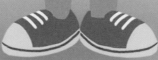

What did this leader say to do?
Can you do it too?

It's so great that there are so many people
playing in the park today!

I see two friends playing hopscotch. You need
good balance to hop on one leg.

Two other friends are taking a bike ride together.
I'm glad to see they are staying on the path and wearing
helmets. That's really important!

Bubbles! I see lots of bubbles in the air.

It's a perfect day for blowing bubbles—
and popping bubbles too!

What's that I hear?
Bounce, bounce, bounce!

A bunch of friends are
busy bouncing balls.

I see a lot of friends playing make-believe. I think I can guess what they're doing.

This girl is going *ZOOM*, like an airplane!

This girl is galloping, just like a horse!

This boy is ROARING like a dinosaur. He's STOMPING like one too!

Beep, beep! This boy is beeping the horn on his truck.

It's a lot quieter over here by the seesaw. These friends are taking turns going up and down.

Did you know that "teeter-totter" is another name for a seesaw? I don't care what you call it—this is a great way to spend time with a friend!

My dog, Lyno, and I had another great day in the park. And it looks like everyone else had one too. Playing with friends is the best!

What's your favorite outdoor game to play with a friend?

Blippi™

Big Order at Blippi's Bakery

Written by Meredith Rusu
Illustrated by Jason Fruchter

Today is a big day! It's the grand opening of my new bakery. Baking makes me happy, and I like to share that happiness with other people.

vegan

gluten-free

nut-&-peanut-free

"Can you make cupcakes for my grandson's birthday party?" one of my customers asks.

"Sure!" I say. "Cupcakes are my specialty."

I just got my first big order. How sweet!

I close the shop so I can concentrate on baking all the cupcakes.

Woah! The party is at three o'clock. That's only four hours from now! I'll have to work fast if I'm going to bake, frost, and deliver everything on time.

There's no time to waste! I hurry to the kitchen. I need to gather all the ingredients. For cupcakes, that means water, eggs, sugar, butter, and of course, lots of flour.

The flour goes into the bowl first.

Poof!

Ha, ha! It's snowing inside!

Next, one at a time, I add the right amount of the rest of the ingredients to the bowl. Then I mix, mix, mix!

All that mixing worked! The ingredients have turned into yummy cupcake batter. Now the batter is ready to be poured into the cupcake pans.

That was so much fun and so easy too!
I just need to place the pans into the oven
to bake-and then I'll clean up the kitchen.

Ding!

My cupcakes are ready! Well, almost ready.
I have to wait until they cool before I can frost them.
You know what's not so easy? Waiting.

What should I do while I wait for the cupcakes to cool?
I know! I'll go home and take Lyno for a walk.

I had such a good time with my best friend!
Now the cupcakes are cool enough to frost. A little frosting here. A little frosting there. A little frosting everywhere!

The cupcakes are ready just in time. The last thing I need to do is place the cupcakes on the cupcake stand.

Uh-oh . . . Where is the cupcake stand?

I've looked everywhere. It isn't on the counter, and it isn't on the shelf.

It isn't in the cupboard or by the sink . . .

Or in the fridge.

I'm going to be late. Where is that cupcake stand?

Phew, I found it! It's in the front window.

I think the stand looks really delicious with lots of birthday cupcakes, don't you?

The cupcakes are stacked. The cupcakes are packed. It's time to get them to the party!

This is my special delivery wagon. It's almost three o'clock! Will I get the cupcakes to the party in time?

Hooray! I am right on time.
Everyone is so happy to see me. And they're
especially happy to see the cupcakes.

"Thank you so much!" says the birthday boy.
"You're welcome!" I say. "It was no trouble
at all. It was a piece of cake. Ha, ha! Make that
a piece of *cup*cake!"

Blippi™
It's Bedtime!

Written by Marilyn Easton
Illustrated by Jason Fruchter

Today, Lyno and I went to the park and played with a friend. We had a fun day! Now it's time to go home.

The day is over. The sun is setting. Soon, the moon will shine brightly in the sky.

Do you see the bird and her
chicks in their nest?
"Good night!" I say.

It's time for Lyno to eat dinner. I pour his favorite food into his dish.
What's *your* favorite food?

While Lyno eats, I check the chart with his bedtime routine. It shows everything we do each night after dinner.

First, I give Lyno a bath. Next, I help him put on his pajamas. Then I brush his teeth. After that, I read one book to Lyno. Then it's time for bed.

Bath

Pajamas

Brush teeth

Book

Bedtime

Hooray! Lyno cleaned his bowl again!
I'm glad he liked his dinner.

It's bath time!

Soap bubbles and bath toys make bath time so much fun!

Lyno likes playing with his toys, especially the rubber duckie.

Can you quack like a duck?

Next, it's time for pajamas.
"Do you want the red pajamas or the purple pajamas tonight?" I ask Lyno.

Ruff! Ruff!

"Ha, ha! Okay, Lyno, the purple ones it is!"
Do you have a favorite pair of pajamas?
What color are they?

Now it's time for the next step in Lyno's bedtime routine.

Lyno has his own special doggy toothpaste.
I squeeze a little bit of it onto his toothbrush.
Then we brush for two minutes!
What does *your* toothpaste taste like?

In the bedroom, I get ready to close the curtains
and say, "Goodbye, moon. See you later, stars."

"Lyno, which book would you like to read? The one about elephants or the one about colors?"

Ruff!

"Elephants sound good to me too. Now climb into your bed."

Do *you* have a favorite book? What is it called?

When we're finished with the book, Lyno is sleepy. He yawns. I yawn too. I tuck his cozy blanket around him.

Lyno closes his eyes.

Do you know how to close your eyes like Lyno?

I turn off the light.
"Good night, Lyno," I whisper. "Sweet dreams."